Not-So-Silly Sausage

D0307556

Northamptonshire
DISCARDED
Libraries

Sch

80 002 542 659

First published 2005
Evans Brothers Limited
2A Portman Mansions
Chiltern Street
London W1U 6NR

Text copyright © Evans Brothers Limited 2005
© in the illustrations Evans Brothers Limited 2005

All rights reserved. No part of this publication
may be reproduced, stored in a retrieval system
or transmitted in any form, or by any means,
electronic, mechanical, photocopying, recording
or otherwise, without the prior permission of
Evans Brothers Limited.

British Library Cataloguing in Publication Data

Gurney, Stella
    Not-so-silly Sausage. - (Twisters)
    1. Children's stories - Pictorial works
    I. Title
    823.9'2 [J]

ISBN 0 237 52875 4

Printed in China by WKT Company Limited

Series Editor: Nick Turpin
Design: Robert Walster
Production: Jenny Mulvanny
Series Consultant: Gill Matthews

Not-So-Silly Sausage

Stella Gurney
and Liz Million

Evans

Northamptonshire Libraries & Information Service	
Peters	24-Mar-05
CF	£3.99

"Look at me!" yelled
Sausage.

"I'm a dolphin!"

6

"Silly Sausage," tutted the
ketchup.

"Silly Sausage," sighed the potatoes.

"A helter-skelter!"

15

16

"Silly Sausage!" sniggered
the beans.

19

"Silly Sausage!"

20

Dan stared. Dan blinked.

22

"Mum!" he shouted.

25

"My sausage is talking!"

"Amazing!" cried Mum.

"Now that's a clever sausage!"

Why not try reading another Twisters book?

Not-so-silly Sausage by Stella Gurney and Liz Million
ISBN 0 237 52875 4
Nick's Birthday by Jane Oliver and Silvia Raga
ISBN 0 237 52896 7
Out Went Sam by Nick Turpin and Barbara Nascimbeni
ISBN 0 237 52894 0
Yummy Scrummy by Paul Harrison and Belinda Worsley
ISBN 0 237 52876 2
Squelch! by Kay Woodward and Stefania Colnaghi
ISBN 0 237 52895 9
Sally Sails the Seas by Stella Gurney and Belinda Worsley
ISBN 0 237 52893 2

If you liked Twisters try a ZigZag!

Dinosaur Planet by David Orme and Fabiano Fiorin
ISBN 0 237 52793 6
Tall Tilly by Jillian Powell and Tim Archbold
ISBN 0 237 52794 4
Batty Betty's Spells by Hilary Robinson and Belinda Worsley
ISBN 0 237 52795 2
The Thirsty Moose by David Orme and Mike Gordon
ISBN 0 237 52792 8
The Clumsy Cow by Julia Moffatt and Lisa Williams
ISBN 0 237 52790 1
Open Wide! by Julia Moffatt and Anni Axworthy
ISBN 0 237 52791 X
Too Small by Kay Woodward and Deborah van de Leijgraaf
ISBN 0 237 52777 4
I Wish I Was An Alien by Vivian French and Lisa Williams
ISBN 0 237 52776 6
The Disappearing Cheese by Paul Harrison and Ruth Rivers
ISBN 0 237 52775 8
Terry the Flying Turtle by Anna Wilson and Mike Gordon
ISBN 0 237 52774 X
Pet To School Day by Hilary Robinson and Tim Archbold
ISBN 0 237 52773 1
The Cat in the Coat by Vivian French and Alison Bartlett
ISBN 0 237 52772 3